PROLOGUE

Wars, at best, are stupid struggles. They are easy to start, easier to keep going, but hard to stop.

This is the story of the three heroes who stopped the Great World War.

To Jane Fonda

THE FORBIDDEN FOREST

Harper & Row, Publishers New York, Hagerstown, San Francisco, London

THE FORBIDDEN FOREST

William Pène du Bois

An Ursula Nordstrom Book

The greatest honor a war hero can receive is to be returned home by special warship.

There were three heroes on the British cruiser *Barham* when it docked in Sydney, Australia. They were known throughout the world as "The Stoppers of the Great War."

One was a bulldog named Buckingham.

Another was a man named Spider Max. He had been a lightweight boxing champion, then went on to boxing a kangaroo.

The third was the mysterious Lady Adelaide. She wore a broad pink sash to which were pinned the four finest medals of the war.

Such was her fame that first a cannon shell, then a hit song, then a popular dance had been named after her.

All three were called "The Lady Adelaide Whizzbang."

9

There was a red carpet leading from the ship's gangplank to a beautiful car. Spider Max stopped on it to read a telegram which a messenger boy had given him.

"Will there be an answer, sir?" asked the messenger boy.

"There will," said Spider Max, "and here it is: Dear Mr. Phineas Barnum STOP Lady Adelaide and I are honored by your generous offer of twenty-five thousand dollars for one boxing exhibition in New York City STOP Regrettably it is out of the question STOP Lady Adelaide has hung up her boxing gloves forever STOP Signed Spider Max."

The beautiful car at the end of the red carpet drove off taking Lady Adelaide back into the jungle.

There, she would be happy to spend the rest of her days with her relatives, the kangaroos, and with her dear friends the wallabies, koala bears, wombats, and forest birds.

Spider Max took Buckingham in a different car to his office. He spent several hours answering questions from the newspapermen, and this is the story which came from the interview.

Spider Max and Lady Adelaide were in Germany near the end of a boxing tour of the world when war was declared.

Lady Adelaide boxed under the name of Battling Sydney. All boxing kangaroos are girls because boy kangaroos become angry and dangerous when teased. Boxing a kangaroo is more of a game than a fight. No one gets hurt.

The night the Great War was to start, Spider Max and Lady Adelaide were boxing in the German city of Aachen.

In the audience sat a man with a red moustache, and next to him sat his bulldog, wearing a cook's hat.

He was a mean-looking man, and his bulldog seemed ashamed to be sitting near him. During the fight, the man stood up with a slingshot and hit Lady Adelaide in the eye with a sour grape.

Lady Adelaide was terribly hurt and, not knowing what she was doing, spun around and bashed her friend Spider Max a terrible wallop with the glove on the end of her tail.

The mean man with the red moustache sat down and roared with laughter. Lady Adelaide heard him and hopped out of the ring, right into the audience, and ran after him. He sped away like the coward he was. Lady Adelaide picked up the slingshot he had left in his seat. She promised herself that one day she would find this terrible man and get her revenge.

That night, Spider Max was shocked to hear that war had been declared. He and Lady Adelaide were in enemy territory. Now, it is impossible for a man to walk down the street with a kangaroo without them both being taken for Australians, and Australians were looked upon as enemies in Germany. Fortunately, they were with a good German friend. It was he who had asked them to come to box in Germany. He liked them and felt that he must look after them. He promised to hide them in his house until the war was over.

Spider Max and Lady Adelaide were given two rooms to live in, with a narrow yard out back where Lady Adelaide could practice jumping.

Lady Adelaide had clothes, dresses she wore in an opening act when she and Spider Max performed in a theater. It was a funny act, based on surprise. Spider Max and Lady Adelaide would enter an elegant restaurant and sit at a table. A white mouse would come trotting in, and at the shout of

"MOUSE, LADY ADELAIDE!"

Lady Adelaide would hop right out of her shoes, straight up to a chandelier.

18

SPIDER MAX PRESENTS

LADY ADELAIDE and the MOUSE

① ③

②

It seemed the war would never end. It dragged on in horror, year after year. Spider Max turned his backyard into a vegetable garden, which kept him busy and fed them both, but in time they became bored and restless. They simply had to get away from their two rooms and garden.

One evening, Lady Adelaide put on a dress, and Spider Max had no sooner led her out into the streets of Aachen, when she stopped short at a restaurant.

Restaurant
Die Große Bombe

There was the face of an ugly man with a red moustache outside.

Adelaide dragged Max inside.

The menu was written on the back of a sign telling people to stay out of a Forbidden Forest or be SHOT AS A SPY WITHOUT TRIAL!

A death warning, on the back of a menu, seemed out of place and cruel to Spider Max.

There was a sad bulldog sitting on a drum in front of a roaring fire. He was turning a roast on a spit with his mouth. The mantelpiece of the fireplace, on which there was a huge cannon shell, was supported by two old cannon barrels.

An ugly German officer with a red moustache, who seemed to own the place, was seated at a table blowing the foam off his beer. He was wearing a spiked helmet and white gloves. He kept shouting at the poor bulldog, "Keep turning, Kaiser! Faster, Kaiser! Turn, you lazy Kaiser dog!"

Lady Adelaide's behavior was both nervous and excited.

Suddenly, she jumped to her feet, hopped across the restaurant, grabbed the German officer's steaming plate of

sauerkraut and sausages, and rubbed it on his nose.

Spider Max ran across the room to see what was going on and received a stiff kick in the behind from the German officer for his efforts. He was later to admit that this was his only contact with the enemy during the war. He was about to use his boxing skills to flatten the German officer when he saw Lady Adelaide go leaping out of the restaurant. Being in enemy territory, he felt it best to leave quickly too.

Fortunately it was quite dark outside, because Lady Adelaide went bounding down the street in giant jumps which had nothing to do with the lovely person she had been pretending to be.

When she reached her room, she could hardly wait to rip off her clothes.

And out of her pocket popped the bulldog, Kaiser. He was still hot from the fire, still wearing his cook's hat, but smiling for the first time in years.

The next morning, in a rather formal ceremony, Spider Max changed the bulldog's name from Kaiser to Buckingham.

Lady Adelaide gave him a British flag she had saved. He grabbed it in his mouth and refused to let it go.

It was a happy day indeed.

Somehow, Spider Max's German host heard about the restaurant scene. "That officer is a dangerous man," he said. "For your own safety, you must leave Aachen at once."

He gave Spider Max a horse and hay wagon. "Hide your animals in the hay, and head for France," he said. "Best of luck!"

Spider Max drove westward throughout the night. The next day he found a place to stay on a French farm, well out of Germany, but much nearer the war. Then, the next morning, to his horror he found that Lady Adelaide and Buckingham had disappeared.

He was later to find that they had hopped over an electrified fence into the Forbidden Forest.

Bekanntmachung!

Jede in diesem Wald erwischte unbefugte Person wird ins Stadtgefängnis geliefert und als Spion ohne Urteilsspruch erschossen werden.

Buckingham led the way, his nose close to the ground, sniffing and grunting like a pig.

Lady Adelaide had taken his flag away from him and hidden it in her pocket.

They soon came across the biggest cannon in history, the terrible Big Bertha. It was used to bombard Paris, eighty miles away, with two-hundred-and-seventy-five-pound shells.

Standing on the bridge, his white-gloved hand pointing to the sky, was none other than the German officer with the red moustache.

When he lowered his hand, the gun would go off, and another shell would be on its way to Paris, a five-minute trip.

Lady Adelaide took her slingshot and the same kind of grape the German officer had used to shoot her.

She aimed carefully for his left eye.

"ZAP!"

A perfect hit. Down came the white hand. Off went the big gun.

There was a terrible explosion. The gun wasn't ready to be fired when the German officer lowered his hand.

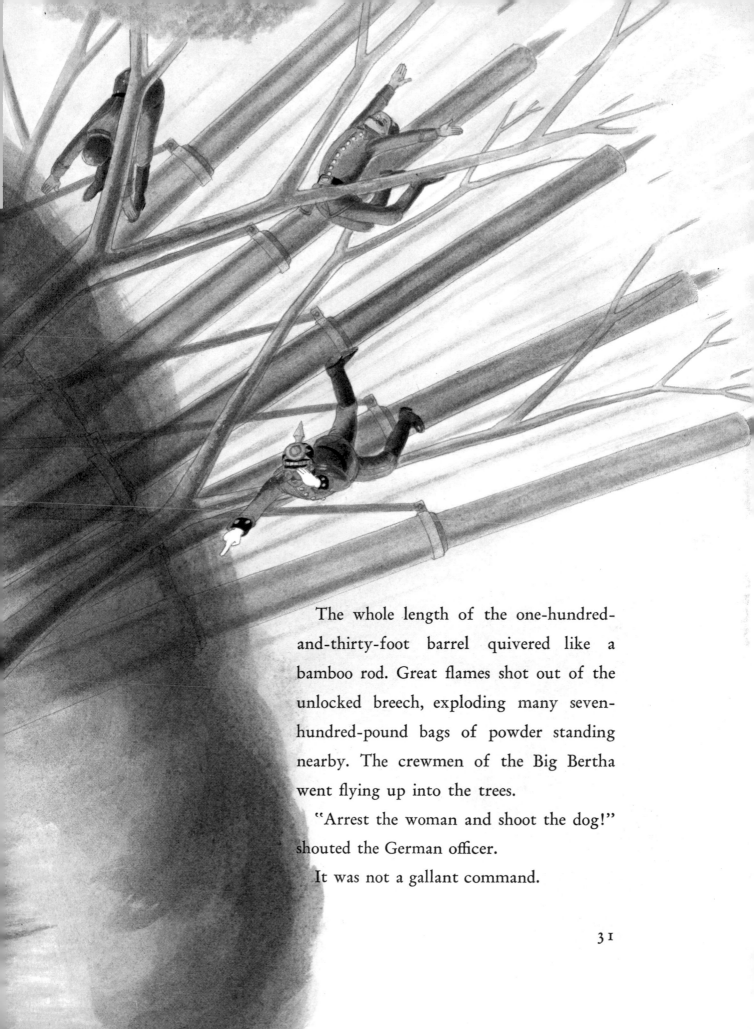

The whole length of the one-hundred-and-thirty-foot barrel quivered like a bamboo rod. Great flames shot out of the unlocked breech, exploding many seven-hundred-pound bags of powder standing nearby. The crewmen of the Big Bertha went flying up into the trees.

"Arrest the woman and shoot the dog!" shouted the German officer.

It was not a gallant command.

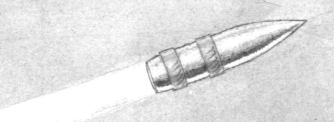

Because of the misfire, a slower shell left the barrel of Big Bertha. It would never reach Paris.

This shell, which later on in history came to be known as "The Lady Adelaide Magic Whizzbang," cut a fantastic path.

Slow to rise in the sky, it first ran into an observation balloon manned by two German spotters with spyglasses. They had been posted to see that no one went near the Forbidden Forest.

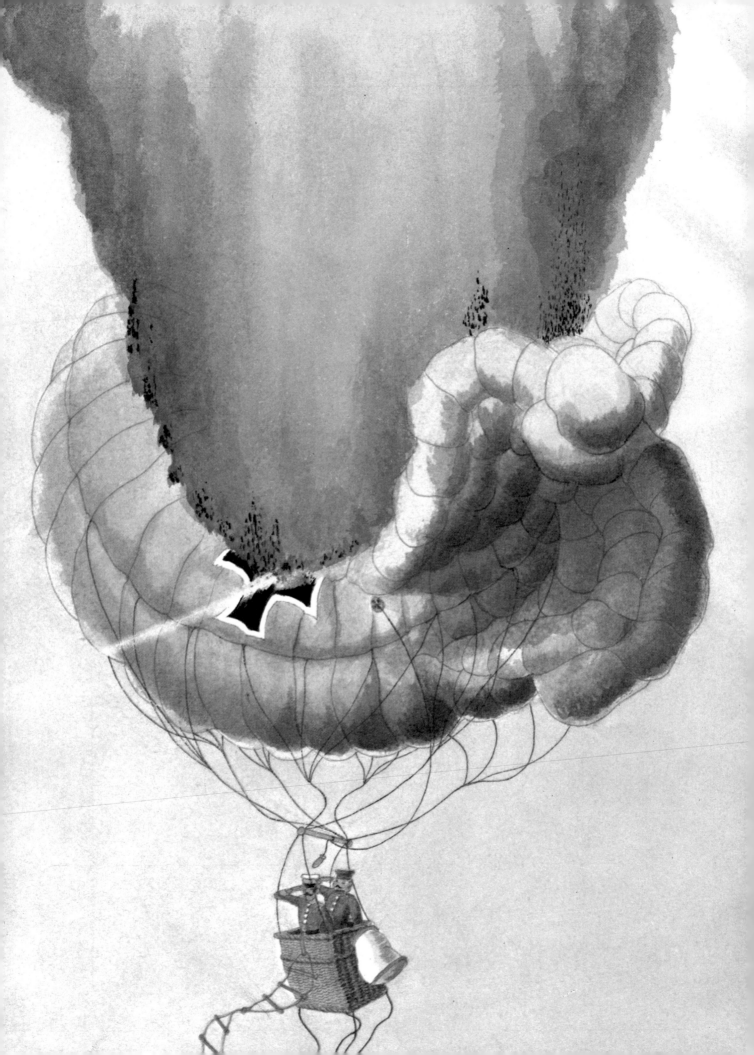

The German observation balloon went down in flames at just the same time German Baron von Wolheim was machine-gunning the wing tips off British Captain Seagraves' airplane.

Hit by "The Lady Adelaide Magic Whizzbang," Baron von Wolheim's airplane exploded like a firecracker.

Meanwhile, back in the Forbidden
Forest, three German soldiers with bay-
onets, and an officer with a saber,
leaped out of trees and arrested Lady
Adelaide.

She was driven off to City Prison,
and condemned to death at sunset.

Buckingham's first thought was to run to Lady Adelaide's rescue; then he decided he'd best race off and get Spider Max instead.

A shot rang out.

It burned the hair on his back.

Buckingham lay down and played dead.

After Baron von Wolheim's plane blew up, Captain Seagraves went about his job, which was to shoot down the German Dirigible L 16.

Hit by "The Lady Adelaide Magic Whizzbang," the Dirigible L 16 split in two right before Captain Seagraves' eyes.

"The Lady Adelaide Magic Whizzbang" was running out of speed. At one point it seemed almost to stop in flight, then came hurtling down to earth.

The greatest German offensive of the war had just begun. The biggest cannon barrage of all times was underway. Gigantic supplies of bullets and bombs had been stored underground.

The most famous German and Austrian generals were up an observation tree with maps and telephones, ready to order the infantry to march on to victory.

Down came "The Lady Adelaide Whizzbang." It cut the observation tree in two, then bounced through the legs of a guard at Gateway 141 on to the world's biggest ammunition dump. There was an odd and sinister silence followed by earth-shattering blasts. The world seemed to be turning itself inside out. The bomb storm lasted a full twenty minutes.

Spider Max heard Buckingham barking and scratching at the door. He opened it fast, and Buckingham ran to the bed where he kept his things, and shook his cook's hat at Spider Max. He's telling me something about Lady Adelaide, thought Spider Max. She can't have gone back to that restaurant. No! The Forbidden Forest! She's been caught and will be shot as a spy!

They ran to the hay wagon. They raced to a city, Buckingham guiding Spider Max with his paws. They stopped at a stone wall on the other side of which Spider Max heard soldiers marching. Buckingham barked and the horse neighed.

Spider Max imagined a German officer pointing with a saber at Lady Adelaide's dear heart and thought, She must remember our mouse act! She must, she must, she must! He pictured her staring into the piercing eyes of the heartless firing squad.

Spider Max waited until he heard two commands, then screamed,

"MOUSE, LADY ADELAIDE!"

A split second before six rifle shots rang out, Lady Adelaide, in a perfect backward somersault, leaped out of her shoes, and up over the wall, landing in the hay wagon.

Lady Adelaide and Buckingham buried themselves in the hay, and Spider Max again headed westward, as fast as his horse could run. He was trying to get away from the German side, even if it meant driving through bullets and bombs on the battlefields. He could hear and smell the war, the sky would light with fire. The countryside was bombed full of holes, and the trees had their tops burnt off. The road was rutted and broken, and he risked hurting his horse or breaking a wagon wheel.

Then, just when he thought the night would never end, there was a moment of absolute silence. Lady Adelaide and Buckingham stuck their heads up through the straw to listen. The horse stopped short and stood still. They seemed to hear church bells, way off in the distance, then more church bells from a different direction, then church bells all around them, some near, some far, some very far away. It was a happy sound, like Christmas.

They drove on.

When the sun came up, they came to a village. A priest had climbed straight up his church steeple to put up a flag.

The war was over!

The villagers greeted Lady Adelaide, Spider Max, and Buckingham with hugs and kisses, food and wine. The horse was given a good meal and a long rest before they drove off to even bigger celebrations, with the biggest of all in Paris.

A few days after they arrived in Paris, Spider Max noticed a strange little sign, in several different languages, posted everywhere. It was a picture of a pink shoe, and the Ministry of War was looking for the woman who owned that shoe. Spider Max, Lady Adelaide, and Buckingham found themselves in a line of women, each of whom had enormous feet. The shoe in the poster looked like one

Lady Adelaide had once owned.

Newspapermen spoke of little else. WHERE IS CINDERELLA FAT FOOT? wrote one. OUR SHY HEROINE WHO WEARS BIG PINK SLIPPERS MUST STEP FORWARD! wrote another.

The reason for the poster was this: a newspaperman was sure the war had been stopped from behind the German lines.

Looking into it, he went first to the blown-up ammunition dump.

He found the German soldier who had been on guard at Gateway 141. He had, by miracle, survived the explosions. He knew everything about shells and identified the one which had bounced between his legs as a Big Bertha shell.

Will the lady who lost this shoe please report to the MINISTRY OF WAR. Exceptional honors await her there. (This is the exact size of the shoe.)

The newspaperman then went into the Forbidden Forest and found that after Big Bertha had blown up, a German officer had ordered his men to "Arrest the woman and shoot the dog!"

The newspaperman next found that a woman had been arrested and a dog had been shot. The woman had been taken to City Prison. He went to City Prison and found that a woman had been shot as a spy, but all that was left of her were two pink slippers. The newspaperman thought that woman must exist and must be found.

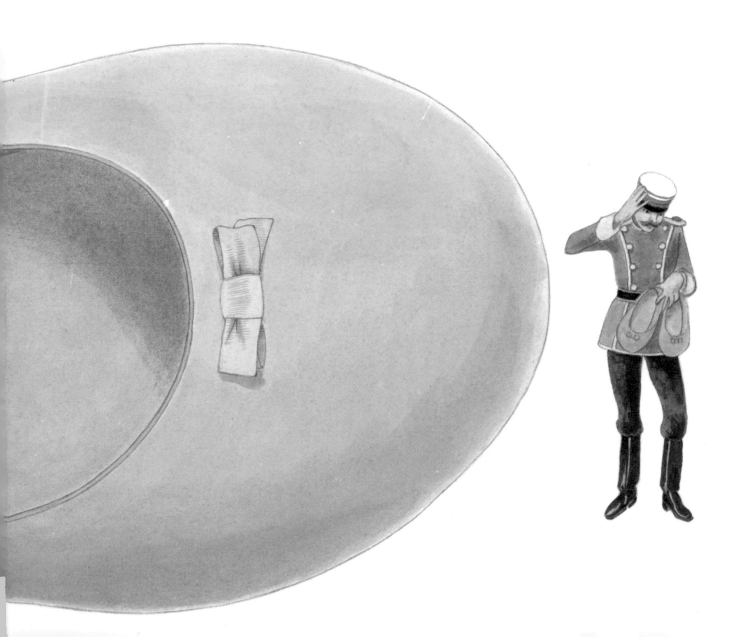

The first of the big-footed ladies in line came back and told the others, "You had better know something about the Forbidden Forest!" None of them seemed to have heard of it. They shrugged their shoulders, turned, and gallumphed home.

Spider Max led Lady Adelaide into a room where she was seated in an armchair. A maid slipped a pink slipper on Lady Adelaide's chubby foot. "A perfect fit!" the maid announced. The greatest heroine of the biggest war had been found.

From the American Government she received The Legion of Merit. From the French Government she received The Croix de Guerre. The British gave her The Order of Distinguished Service, and the Italians gave her The Order of Saint Maurice and Lazare.

She also got many many kisses on both cheeks.